Where the Adventure is

By Jared Goodykoontz

LABC Book #1

D1511672

This book is dedicated to:

Charlotte - my beautiful, inspiring and supportive wife.
I couldn't do the things I do without you!

Annelise - my curious, hilarious, spunky daughter. I love you because you're you!

My friends, coworkers, and family -
for supporting me and helping me grow

The LDBB Admins - for finding many ways to say "yes" to my dreams

Ollie & Gerald - friends forever

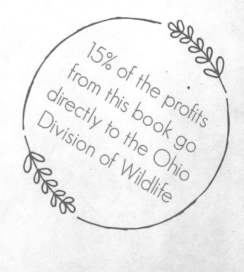

15% of the profits from this book go directly to the Ohio Division of Wildlife

About the Author

Jared Goodykoontz loves to go outside and enjoy God's creation... on his own, with his loved ones, and with his students. He teaches Pre-K in Columbus, Ohio and runs the Little Adventures, Big Connections Nature Program with 100+ kiddos every week.

Somewhere, in an old Ohio field, there is a bus.
Under that bus live two mushrooms: the sister named
Mooshy Moo and the brother named Grumpus.

Mooshy Moo was a bit persistent.

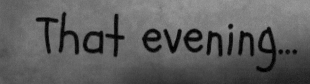

That evening...

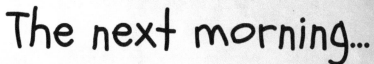

The next morning...

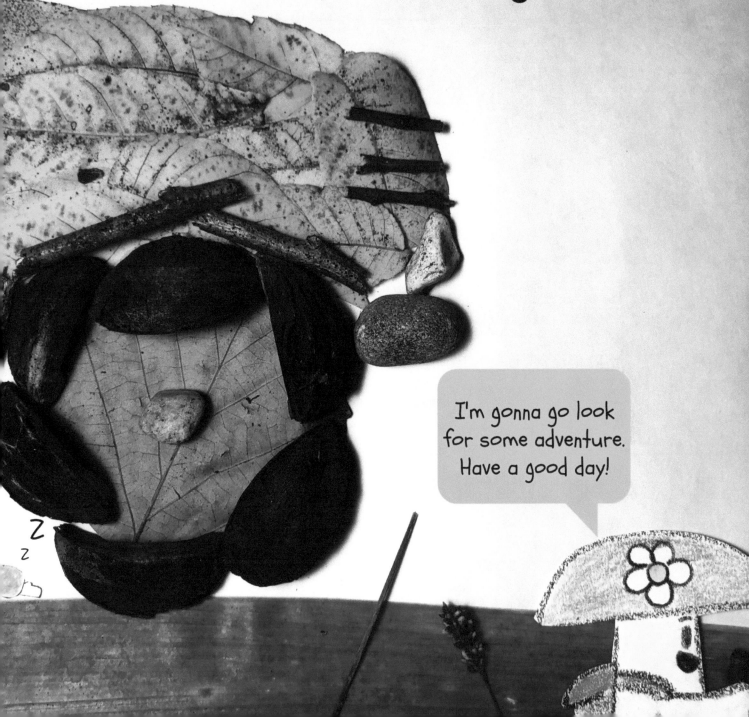

Mooshy Moo stopped and sat down.
Grumpus waited to see what was going to happen.
He waited... and waited... and waited......... and WAITED.

Oh, hi Chip.
sniff
HI!!!
!
Hey... where's he going?
scurry
I think you scared him. It's okay. Come sit with me.

As Chip the chipmunk sprang away, Grumpus sat in stunned silence for a few minutes.

Mooshy Moo worried that he was upset.

Finally, he let Mooshy Moo know what he was thinking...

That.
Was...

spring

As the sun began to set, the mushroom siblings trekked back home to their bus, talking along the way.

Grumpus wondered who else he could share it with.

"Fireflies!" Grumpus whispered excitedly.

As the moon rose, one friendly firefly landed in Grumpus' hands. He told his new friend everything.

Grumpus still wants to be where the adventure is, but now he knows he doesn't have to go very far at all.

Extension Ideas
Try these out on your own and with your family and friends!

Magic Spot
— • ▌ • —

Find somewhere outside where you can comfortably sit for awhile and experience the world around you- the sights, the sounds, the sensations, the smells... everything! Sometimes you can just take it all in at once, and sometimes you can focus on one sense at a time.

Try to pick a spot that you can get to easily and often (perhaps your backyard or a nearby park).
The more often you go, the more adventures will come to you!

Nature Journal
— • ▌ • —

Once you start regularly visiting your Magic Spot, you'll begin to experience all sorts of adventures- meeting wild animal brothers and sisters, hearing new bird and bug songs, smelling new smells and much more!

You'll want to keep track of all these wonderful discoveries in a journal through writing or drawing... you can make one yourself or just use one you already have. Try to journal after each experience in nature.

Here's the most important part: share!
Share your stories with people you love... you'll all benefit!

Explore
facebook.com/jgoodstories
for more Mooshy Moo
& Grumpus books etc!

RECIPE

Can you find the following bits throughout the book?

~Lily Leaves ~Ironweed Blossoms ~Oak Leaves ~Watercolor Pencils

~Basswood Leaves ~Various Stones and Pebbles ~Colored Pencils

~Moss ~Dirt ~Dandelion Leaves ~ Watercolor Paper ~Chicory

~Red Clover ~Bark ~Twigs ~Crayon ~Marigolds ~Walnut Leaves

~Geo Sans Light, Shadows Into Light Two & Schoolbell fonts

~Various Grasses, Rushes & Sedges ~Aster Buds ~Patience

CPSIA information can be obtained
at www.ICGtesting.com
Printed in the USA
BVHW020758150120
R10592600001B/R105926PG569262BVX3B/2/P